By
Judith C. Owens-Lalude

AnikePress - Worldwide Publisher
Henderson, Nevada, USA

Orders: AnikePress.com

ISBN: 978-0-9848203-7-5
LCCN: 2015905155

Revised: 2022

Book cover layout and illustrations
by Judith C. Owens-Lalude

What's inside:
Over 120 **P** words
Nearly 150 science facts
Guide for Teachers & Parents
Subject-based activities that support school curricula

To contact the author or receive information about
book signings and programs that accompany
PEAS AND THE POPOVER:

http://jcamilleculturalacademy.com
http://JudithCamille.com
jclalude@gmail.com

PEAS
AND THE POPOVER
and a

Guide for Teachers & Parents

Peas and the Popover is a fun read-aloud for young people and is inclusive of a learning guide that can be used as an early introduction to mathematics and science.

PEAS
AND THE POPOVER

Papa asks **Peter** to **pick peas**. **Peter** grabs his cap. He heads toward the vegetable **patch**. At the **patch**, he **puts** his **pea-picking pail** down next to his knee. **Peter pretends** to be a farmer. He **picks peas** from the vine. He **puts** the **peas** into a **pail**.

When he reaches for another **pea**, the earth beside his knee **puffs** up. It forms a mound. **Peter** leans back. He **perches** on his heels. He **ponders**, what could it **possibly** be? **Peter** lowers his head and **peeps** at the mound. Up **pops** Ernie, the earthworm. Ernie shakes dirt off the tip of his **prostomium**.

"Good morning, **Peter**," he says.

Peter asks Ernie, "Are you looking for water to wet your soil?"

"No, **Peter**. I want to see who is **picking** my **peas**."

Satisfied, Ernie **pushes** his body back into his hole. **Peter** continues to **pick peas**. He **picks** until his **pea-picking pail** is full.

Back home, **Peter** sits on a bench. He **puts** the **pea-picking pail** between his knees. He shells the **peas** one **pea pod** at a time. When **Papa** walks by, he smiles at **Peter**. "This will be a **perfect** meal, **Peter**," says **Papa**.

Papa boils water in a **purple pot**. He **pours** the **peas** from the **pea-picking pail** into the cooking **pot** full of water. **Papa puts** a top on the **pot**. Steam hisses loud. It **puffs** out from underneath the lid. The top rattles and clanks.

"It won't be long before the **peas** are done," says **Papa** to **Peter**.

While **Papa** waits for the **peas** to cook, he bakes **popovers** for **Peter** to eat with the **peas**.

Then **Papa places** a serving bowl on the table. **Pretty pink** and **purple pansies** and **petunias** are **painted** on it. **Papa pours** the **peas** into the bowl. He dots the **peas** with butter. Then, he sprinkles them with salt. **Papa** even teases the **peas** with a **pinch** of white **pepper**.

At half **past** two, **Papa** says, "Come, **Peter**. The **peas** are ready to eat. Sit here, son."

Papa piles plenty of **peas** on **Peter's plate.** He **puts** a **puffy popover** next to them. **Peter picks** up his fork to eat his **peas**. The **peas** roll away from **Peter** and some off his **plate**.

"Ooops!" cried **Peter**.

The **peas plummet** to the floor. **Piper**, his **puppy**, **paws** the peas. **Pammy**, his kitten, **pounces** on the **peas**. **Peter** lifts his fork. He **pushes** it underneath his **peas.** He lifts his fork up off his **plate**. He tries to eat his **peas**. Up, up, and away they fly. Then, the **peas pour** down on him.

Peter chases the green **peas** across his **plate**. They jump off the edge of it. Some some of the **peas** drop to the floor, *plump, plump-plump.* **Pammy** and **Piper** nose-**push peas** across the floor. The other **peas** roll out the door.

To not be out done by the **peas**, **Peter** sighs and says, "I'll try again."

He stacks the **peas** back on his fork. He lifts them up off his **plate**. He lowers his head. His eyes cross when he hurries to eat his **peas**. When he uncrosses them, there are no **peas** on his fork.

"I won't give up!" **Peter** says.

Peter pinches the **popover's** cap off. Afterward, he **pinches** each **pea**. One by one, he **plops** a **pea** into the **popover**. To his delight, the **peas** are trapped. He eats the **popover** full of **peas**.

Exhausted, **Peter** slumps in his chair. He rests his head next to his **plate**. **Peter** dreams that he chases the **peas**, and the **peas** chase him. They catch him. The **peas pull Peter** into a **pink**, **puffy popover** full of buttered **peas**.

The End

GUIDE FOR

TEACHERS
&
PARENTS

for
3-year olds
and up

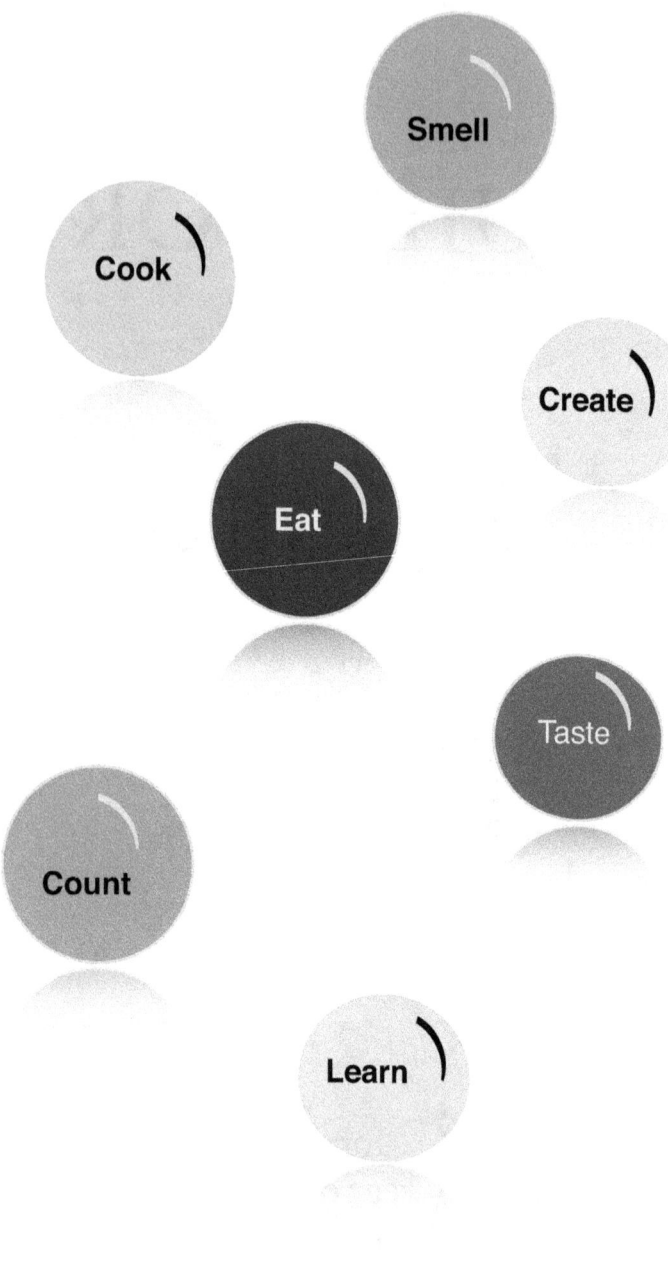

Table of Contents

Introduction

120 **P** Words … 8

Science of Green Peas

Earthworms … 12

PEAS 13

Peas for Nutrition … 14

Popovers in Science … 15

More Food Science … 16

Food & Mathematics … 18

Peas & Numbers … 20

Mathematical Words … 22

Language Arts & Activities … 23

Visual Art

Activity I: Color the **Ps** … 25

Activity II: Draw **Ps** … 26

Activity III: Using **P** Colors … 26

Activity IV: Paste **Ps** … 27

Activity V: Make a Book … 28

Activity VI: Make a Whatnot Box … 28

P Fonts … 29

P Food Art

Activity I: Food + Science = Knowledge … 30

Activity II: Draw, Paint and Cut … 30

Activity III: Make a **P** Wind Charm … 31

Trace a **P** … 33

P Puzzle … 35

Popover Nutrition … 36

Popover Recipe … 37

About the Author … 39

INTRODUCTION

The **Guide for Teachers & Parents** is designed to accompany the story, *Peas and the Popover.* The lessons support existing school curricula and will perk up a science or mathematics lesson, making education meaningful while creating positive learning.

P is a fun letter to learn about. It works well with words and rhymes. *Peas and the Popover* is a whimsical story that teaches pre-readers about the letter **P**. Fun reading promotes faster learning. Children don't easily forget what they learn if it makes them laugh.

The **Guide for Parents & Teachers** is complete with activities that span the curricula. The lessons are created to be used with an interdisciplinary format and are intended to generate dialogue that stimulates learning.

Peas and the Popover is a story with lessons about green peas and earthworms:

1. Pea pods grow on a vine.

2. Pea pods are a fruit.

3. Seeds inside the pea pod are eaten as a vegetable.

4. Peas are part of the legume family.

5. Peas are usually green.

6. Earthworms live in wet soil.

7. Popovers are a soft, quick bread. Yeast is not needed to make them rise.

120 P Words

Animals	Adjectives
1. panther	1. pair
2. parakeet	2. pale
3. parrot	3. pastel
4. peacock	4. patchy
5. pelican	5. perfect
6. penguin	6. perky
7. pheasant	7. petite
8. pica	8. pink
9. pigeon	9. plain
10. pit bull	10. pleasant
11. platypus	11. plenty
12. polar bear	12. plump
13. polecat	13. popular
14. pony	14. positive
15. poodle	15. pretty
16. porcupine	16. prim
17. prairie dog	17. puffy
18. puffin	18. pure
19. pug	19. purple
20. puppy	20. pushy

Foods

1. pancake
2. peach
3. peanut
4. pear
5. peas
6. pecan
7. peppermint
8. pie
9. pizza
10. plum
11. popcorn
12. popover
13. popsicle
14. pork
15. porridge
16. potato
17. poultry
18. pretzel
19. prunes
20. pudding

Objects

1. package
2. pail
3. pan
4. pearl
5. pencil
6. person
7. piano
8. picture
9. pillow
10. pipe
11. plane
12. plate
13. platter
14. pole
15. poncho
16. pot
17. pouch
18. prize
19. purse
20. puzzle

Places	Things to Do
Places	**Things to Do**
1. palace	1. paddle
2. pantry	2. paint
3. paradise	3. pat
4. Paris	4. peel
5. park	5. peep
6. pasture	6. perch
7. peninsula	7. pick
8. Peru	8. picnic
9. Philadelphia	9. pitch
10. Phoenix	10. plant
11. pit	11. play
12. plateau	12. plow
13. planet	13. poke
14. pool	14. polish
15. porch	15. pound
16. port	16. pour
17. Portland	17. powder
18. Portugal	18. pretend
19. pothole	19. punish
20. prairie	20. push

Science

Art

GREEN
PEAS

Mathematics

EARTHWORM

1. Ernie the earthworm was asked if he needed water to wet his dirt. Earthworms live in wet soil.

2. Ernie the earthworm shakes sand and dirt from his prostomium, (pro•sto•mi•um). This is a lobe at the very tip of the earthworm's head.

3. The prostomium hangs over the mouth of the earthworm to allow it to open cracks and make tunnels in the soil.

4. The earthworm has no teeth to work with. It has only the prostomium.

5. Earthworms help peas grow by tunneling through and loosening the soil around their roots (a form of irrigation).

PEAS
pisum sativum
(small spherical seeds)
Seed or seed-pod of the pod fruit

1. Peas are a low-growing vine plant.

2. The pea plant is a flowering plant.

3. Each pea pod contains several peas.

4. Green peas inside the pea pods are popped out and cooked to eat. Some are eaten raw.

5. Pea seeds are spherical (round). They can roll around on a flat surface.

PEAS FOR NUTRITION
World's Healthiest Food

Peas are a good source of energy and nutrition. They contain:

Vitamins
1. **A** to help keep eyes and skin healthy

2. **B-1** for healthy skin, hair, muscles, and bones

3. **B-2** helps keep the skin, hair, blood, and brain healthy

4. **B-6** helps keep the heart healthy

5. **C** helps fight infection

6. **K** helps blood to clot

Minerals

1. **Copper** helps keep blood and nerves healthy

2. **Protein** is a body builder

3. **Iron** is good for the blood and energy

4. **Zinc** keeps body cells healthy

These are not all of the food nutrients or all of their functions.

POPOVERS IN SCIENCE

1. Popover is a soft, quick bread.
    It rises without yeast.

2. Popovers are baked in a very
    hot oven that produces dry heat.

3. The hole in the center of the
    popover is created by steam that
    is generated when the batter gets
    hot.

4. Popovers are full of protein and
    carbohydrate. They can be a good
    source of energy.

MORE FOOD SCIENCE

Reread *Peas and the Popover* aloud to your young audience. Afterward, set up an experiment to show how green peas grow.

Supplies: Aprons, drop cloth, small planting pots, potting soil, miniature spades, seeds, spices, butter, olive oil, water, and paper towels

1.   Using a drop cloth, prepare a work area. Fill pots with soil.

2.   Plant seeds in the pots of soil, water them, and watch the peas grow. Record what happens.

3.   Pick, shell, steam, season, and eat the peas. Note the skin, texture and taste of the peas.

WARNING: *Young children can swallow and choke on dry peas.*

Bake Popovers

See recipe on page *37.* Let an adult help.
1.   Watch the popovers rise.
2.   When done, let them cool.
3.   Open the top and peer inside.
4.   Note the cavity created by the heat and steam.
5.   Describe the flavor, smell, and texture of the popover.
6.   Make a list of foods that can be put into a popover and eaten.

Listed below are other foods that can roll around like green peas:
Blueberries, boiled egg yolks, cherries, cherry tomatoes, grapes, and more

Can you think of other foods that are round? If so, list them below:
1. _____   3. _____
2. _____   4. _____

On a sheet of paper draw pictures of your favorite round foods.

FOOD
&
MATHEMATICS

Compare different types of peas and note the different pea sizes

Supplies: Peas (canned, cooked, frozen, or dried), bowls, metric ruler, measuring tools, plate, spoons, safety scissors, and paper towels.

Measuring tools can be:
> Kitchen spoons
> Measuring cups
> Measuring spoons
> Ramekins
> Small tea cups
> Shot glasses

🌱 Open containers of peas (do not mix them):
> Green peas
> Split peas
> Black-eyed peas
> Chickpeas

🌱 Cook peas one pouch or can per pot. Do not mix the peas.

1. Using the same measuring tool, scoop peas from each pot of peas. Put one scoop in each pot, separate bowls, or on plates. Do not mix the peas.

2. Count the cooked peas in each group.

3. Record the number of peas counted in each group.

4. Make a bar graph and a pie graph using the numbers of peas in each measured group.

5. Us pink and purple colors to create the graphs.

Before starting:
Parents and teachers should do the experiments before working with young children. Select measuring tools according to the child's skill level and age. A larger measuring tool requires more counting and figuring. This is good for older children, but might be troubling for younger ones.

WARNING: *Young children can swallow and choke on dry peas.*

PEAS & NUMBERS

1. Scoop up peas with a measuring tool. Count the peas as you put them in a bowl. Record the number. This number is a **sum**.

2. Divide the peas into clusters of 10. How many groups do you have? How many peas are left over? Those peas are the **remainder**.

3. Put two more peas in each pile. Now each pile has 12 peas, or a dozen, in it. How many dozens did the peas make? How many peas are left over? Those peas are the **remainder**.

4. **Subtract** the number of leftover peas from the total number of peas. That is the **difference** or the **remainder**.

5. How many peas are in each group of peas. The total number of peas is the **sum**.

6. Subtract the number of leftover peas from each group. These peas are the **difference** or **remainder**.

7. **Add** the remainder of peas, from each group together. The peas are now a **sum**.

8. Use a metric ruler to measure the peas, popover, bowl, and a plate. Record the results.

To compare results, use the same tool to measure the different types of peas.

MATHMATICAL
WORDS

Add is to create more by putting more peas in a group.

Subtract is to take peas away from a group of peas.

Remainder is the number of peas leftover after some of the peas are removed from the group.

Difference is the number of peas in one group that is less or greater than the number of peas in the other group.

Sum is all the peas in a bowl, pot, measuring tool, cup, or on a plate.

LANGUAGE ARTS
&
ACTIVITIES

1. Make a list of **P** words.

2. Write a story using **P** words.

3. Give each child a half-sheet of newspaper. Have them circle or highlight words starting with the letter **P**.

4. Make several copies of the same page from a magazine. Give a page to each child. See who can find the most **P** words in one minute.

5. Give each child a copy of the *Peas and the Popover* story. Have them to:
    a. Underline adjectives starting with the letter **P.**
    b. Circle the verbs that start with the letter **P**.

c. Box objects that begin
with the letter **P**.

6. Create a menu with foods that
begin with the letter **P**.

7. Use a **P** word to describe the
difference noticed after the
peas are cooked.

8. Using the list below, write
complete sentences with each
word, containing at least one **P**
word:

    a. Bicycle
    b. Book
    c. Chair
    d. Dog
    e. Doll
    f. Teddy Bear
    g. Tree

Note: To help, use the lists on pages
8, 9, and 10 for word and ideas.

VISUAL ARTS

Activity I: Color the "P"

Make me pretty
Make me pleasing
Color me pink
Color me purple

Activity II: Draw Ps

Supplies: White butcher, construction, or copy paper, and safety scissors

1.   Give each child a blank sheet of paper.

2.   Have them fold the sheet in half and then in half again. Now there are four squares.

3.   Draw a **P** in quarter sections and color each in a **P** color.

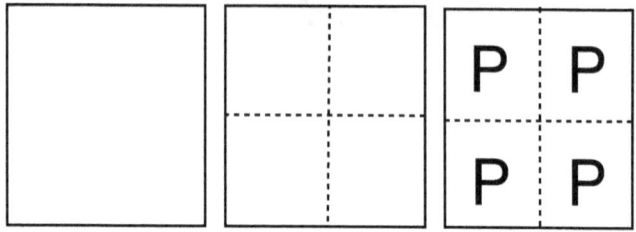

Activity III: Using P Colors . . .

1.   Give each child one sheet of folded paper that has four **P**s on it. (see figure above)

2. Color the **P** letters using purple and pink coloring tools.

3. Give each child a second sheet of blank white paper.

4. Cut the **P**s out.

5. Paste the **P**s on the second sheet of white paper to create a design. (see the **P** flower on page 31)

Activity IV: Make Greeting Cards

Give each child 2 sheets of white art or copy paper and one sheet of pink and one of purple paper, both folded in half.

1. On one sheet of white paper, trace **P**s and cut them out.

2. Paste the **P**s on the front sides of the folded colored papers.

3. Paste a sheet of white paper inside of the folded colored papers.

4. Write a greeting using a **P** word.

Makes 2 cards

Activity V: Make a Book

1. Fold 2 sheets of white paper in half. From another sheet of paper, cut out a few white **Ps.**

2. Fold a sheet of pink or purple colored paper in half to create the front and back book cover.

3. Paste the **P**s on the front cover.

4. Staple or glue the white sheets of paper inside the folded colored paper to create a book.

Activity VI: Make a Whatnot Box

1. Draw or trace **P**s and green peas on white paper.
2. Color them pink and purple.
3. Cut out **P**s and green peas.
4. Paste them on a box with a lid to create a design on it. (See pg.31)
5. Mix and match the colors.

P FONTS

$\mathcal{P}$

FOOD ART

Identify foods that start with the letter P. Use the **Foods** listed on page 9.

Activity I: Food + Science = Knowledge

1. Gather foods that begin with the letter **P**.

2. Use **P** words to tell about the foods (color, taste, texture) and what you can do with the foods (eat, roll, toss).

3. Select, draw, and paint foods.

Activity II: Draw, Paint, and Cut

1. Draw a bowl on art paper. Paint it purple.
2. Cut out the bowl.
3. Cut out **P** foods from magazines.
4. Paste them on the purple bowl.

An old bowl can be used instead of the paper one to create a collage on.

Activity III: Make a Wind Charm

1. Tie different lengths of strings to a wire coat hanger.

2. Draw large **P**s. Color them pink and purple.

3. Cut out the **P**s and **P** foods. Use the list on page 9 for suggestions.

4. Paste the cutout **P**s and **P** foods (page 9) to the ends of the strings.

5. Dangle the coat hanger high on a door frame or a rafter. Watch the **P**s and **P** foods spin and swing about.

Pea Flower

ART

In the box below make funny **P**s

Trace the **P** with your:

Finger
Pencil
Pen
Crayon
Marker

ART

In the box below create art with **P**s

(see figure on page 31)

$\mathcal{P}$

PUZZLE

Circle the **P**s below

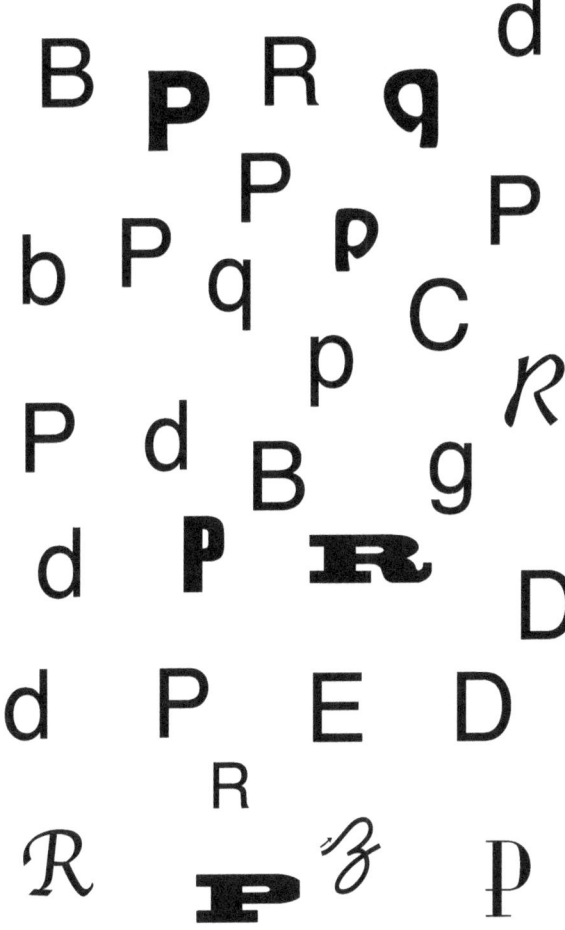

Nutritional Facts for one popover:
154 calories, 7 gm total fat (2 gm saturated fat).
74 mg cholesterol, 130 mg sodium, 17gm
carbohydrates, 1gm fiber, 5gm protein.

Makes 6 popovers

POPOVERS

Always wash your hands and finger nails before preparing food.

Preheat oven to 400°F (fahrenheit)

Ingredients
    1   tablespoon shortening
    2   beaten eggs
    1   cup milk
    1   tablespoon cooking oil
    1   cup flour
  1/4 teaspoon salt

1. Using 1/2 teaspoon shortening for each cup, grease the bottom of a six-ounce custard cup or cups of a popover pan. Place the custard cups on a 15x10x1 inch backing pan: set aside.

2. In a mixing bowl, use a wire whisk or rotary beater to beat eggs, milk, and oil until combined. Add flour and 1/4 teaspoon salt; mix until smooth. Do not overbeat.

3. Fill the prepared cups 1/2 full with batter. Bake in a 400°F oven for about 40 minutes or till very firm.

4. Turn the oven off. Using oven mittens, remove the popover pan from the oven; prick each with a fork or toothpick to let the steam escape.

Judith C. Owens-Lalude

. . .with her dog, Mickey,
a gift from Grandmother
when Mickey was a

PUPPY

ABOUT THE AUTHOR
Judith C. Owens-Lalude

Owens-Lalude is a graduate from Kentucky State University, Frankfort, Kentucky, and has a Master's degree in education from California State University Long Beach, California. Owens-Lalude is married to A. O'tayo Lalude, M.D. They have two sons who are engineers and international businessmen.

Owens-Lalude's special interest is in the education of students around the world. She traveled to Europe where she explored the impact of language on children as they interacted with others from different cultures; Nigeria to study family and culture; and then to the Fourth World Conference on Women, Beijing, China, 1995.

www.ingramcontent.com/pod-product-compliance
Lightning Source LLC
Chambersburg PA
CBHW071226170626
46809CB00005BA/1957

* 9 7 8 0 9 8 4 8 2 0 3 7 5 *